SELECT
EDITIONS

Farm Tales

WRITTEN BY MOIRA BUTTERFIELD

ILLUSTRATED BY COLIN PETTY

CONTENTS

WHAT THE CAT DID

There was once a farm where a dog and a cat lived. The dog ran around all day being very busy, but the cat spent most of her day lying in the sun.

"I'm much better at everything than you," said the dog to the cat. "You're just a lazy, useless lump and I do all the work around here. I don't know why the farmer bothers to keep you!"

The cat did not reply. She just wiggled her whiskers, which annoyed the dog very much.

"I can bark and you can't," said the dog. "Woof, woof!" He ran around the farmyard barking loudly.

The cat did not reply. She just winked one eye, which annoyed the dog even more!

"I can wag my tail much faster than you," said the dog. Swish, swish! He wagged his tail as fast as he could.

The cat did not reply. She just licked her paws, which annoyed the dog even more!

"I can round up sheep and you can't!" said the dog. He ran into the field and rounded up all the sheep as quickly as he could.

The cat did not reply. She just padded slowly over to the farmhouse and jumped up on the farmer's lap.

"What a beautiful cat you are," said the farmer, and he stroked her ears just the way she liked.

The poor dog was worn out and muddy. He was so tired that he didn't have the energy to jump up on the farmer's lap!

"You see, silly dog," purred the cat. "I can do NOTHING much better than you."

The worn-out dog sat panting on the floor, while the cat curled up in the farmer's lap, where she was very comfortable and warm. Who do YOU think was the cleverest animal that day?

FARMER BROWN AND THE TALENT CONTEST

One day, Mr. Brown the farmer got a letter through the post. It said:

Dear Mr. Brown,
Tomorrow we are holding a village fair and a talent contest. Prizes will be awarded to contestants who show special talent.

The letter was signed by the judge of the contest, who wrote another line on the bottom:

P.S.: Animals can enter, too.

"I'd like my animals to win a prize!" said the farmer to his wife. "I'll gather them together in the farmyard straight away. Then I'll see what they can do!"

The farmer called his cows, his sheep and his hens into the farmyard.

"Mmm, you don't look a very talented bunch," he said. "Never mind, I've had an idea. I want you all to sing a song. That will win prizes!"

The farmer stood in front of his animals ready to conduct them with a stick.

"I want you to sing 'Baa, baa, black sheep'," he said. "Are you ready? One, two, three . . ."

All the animals tried to sing as loudly as they could.

"Moo, baa, cluck! Moo, baa, cluck . . ." What a terrible noise they made!

"Stop!" shouted the farmer. "That was the worst song I've ever heard!"

"What a silly man you are," said the farmer's wife, who was watching. "Animals can't sing songs!"

"Never mind, I've had another idea," said the farmer. "I want you all to do a dance. THAT will win prizes!"

The farmer stood in front of his animals, ready to show them how to dance.

"I want you to copy what I do," he said. "Are you ready? One, two, three . . ."

All the animals tried to follow what the farmer did. They got into a dreadful mess! The cows bumped into the sheep. The sheep turned the wrong way round and the hens ran round in circles!

"Stop!" shouted the farmer. "That was the worst dance I've ever seen!"

"What a silly man you are," said the farmer's wife, who was watching. "Animals can't dance!"

The farmer began to get grumpy.

"I give up with these stupid creatures," he said to his wife. "We'll have to do without any prizes, unless you can think of something better." He stomped off to the farmhouse in a temper.

"Don't worry," the farmer's wife said to the animals. "I've had an idea." She whispered to them each in turn and then sent them off to bed.

The next morning, the farmer's wife got up very early and disappeared into the farmyard. After a while she came back to have some breakfast with the grumpy farmer.

"Are you coming to the fair today?" she asked him.

"No fear," he replied. "We'll never win any prizes."

"Please yourself," said the farmer's wife, and she drove off to the village. The farmer didn't know that her car was loaded with lots of goodies to enter into the talent contest!

The farmer's wife entered a basket of eggs from the hen.

"Laying eggs is a very special talent," said the judge. "I'll give your hen a prize!"

The farmer's wife entered a pail of cream from the cows.

"Making cream is a very special talent," said the judge. "I'll give your cows a prize!"

The farmer's wife entered a bail of wool from the sheep.

"Making wool is a very special talent," said the judge. "I'll give your sheep a prize!"

The farmer was very, very surprised when his wife came home and showed him the prizes.

"However did you do it?" he asked.

"Well, I used a very special talent that no-one else has got around here!" chuckled the wife. "I used my brains!"

THE NAUGHTY MISCHIEF-MAKER

There was once a farmer who was very proud of his tidy farm. Each night he put his cows in their barn and carefully shut the door.

But one morning, he came outside and found the door open. The cows were in the farmyard, in the lanes and even in the farmer's own garden, where they were busy munching his flowers!

That same day, the farmer put his hay neatly inside the haybarn and carefully shut the door.

But when he came back from a trip to his fields, he found the door open. The hay was spread all over the farmyard, and it was even in the farmer's kitchen!

That very afternoon, the farmer milked his cows and put the milk in a tidy row of pails.

He turned his back for just a moment, and when he looked back again the pails had fallen over. The milk spilt over the floor and it even lapped the farmer's boots!

The farmer went to see his wise old Grandad and asked him what to do about all the trouble.

"It sounds like there is someone very naughty on your farm," said Grandad. "I know just how to catch a mischief-maker! I'll come and show you tomorrow."

The next day, the farmer's wise old Grandad arrived with a truck full of shiny apples.

"These apples are the best ones I've ever seen," he said. "Your naughty mischief-maker will eat them all, mark my words!"

He parked his truck in the farmyard.

"Now, let's go back into the farmhouse and wait until nightfall. We'll creep out again when it's dark," he whispered. "I'm sure we'll catch your mischief-maker then!"

When darkness fell, the farmer and his wise old Grandad crept out into the farmyard. Sure enough, someone had eaten all the apples. A trail of apple cores led across the yard to the haybarn.

The farmer and his wise old Grandad tiptoed to the door of the barn. They heard a loud snoring noise coming from inside.

"There's your mischief-maker," whispered Grandad. "He's eaten so many apples that he has fallen fast asleep. Let's surprise him!"

Grandad flung open the door.

"Boo!" he shouted, at the top of his voice, and he rushed in with the farmer behind him.

There was the farm scarecrow, asleep on the hay! He had a terrible fright and he jumped up, scattering apple cores all around the barn!

"So it was YOU who was so naughty, scarecrow," cried the farmer. "You should be ashamed of yourself, making such a mess! Will you promise never to be naughty again?"

"You'd better promise, scarecrow, or I'll be back to catch you!" said Grandad.

The scarecrow was very sorry. He never behaved badly again, and he never ate another apple as long as he lived!

THE LITTLE TRACTOR

One day Farmer Brown went to a tractor sale. He passed all the biggest tractors and stopped by the smallest one.

"You'll do nicely for what I want," he said, and he drove the little tractor home.

"Hurrah, I've got a job!" thought the little tractor to herself. "I wonder what the farmer will use me for. I'm only small, but I'll try my hardest."

Farmer Brown parked the little tractor alongside some much bigger farm machines.

"Tomorrow Farmer Brown is going to plough his fields. We'll be very busy," they said.

The next day, Farmer Brown ploughed his fields. He used some of the big machines, but not the little tractor.

"Tomorrow Farmer Brown is going to sow some seed. We'll be very busy," said the big machines.

The next day, the farmer sowed some seed. He used the big machines, but not the little tractor.

"I wonder if he'll use me tomorrow . . ." sighed the little tractor.

But the days went by and Farmer Brown did not start up her engine. The grass started to grow up around her wheels and every day the farm cat slept under her in the shade.

"Perhaps the farmer has changed his mind about me," thought the little tractor sadly. "He doesn't think I'm big enough to use for any work . . ."

"Tomorrow Farmer Brown is on holiday," said the big machines one evening. "We won't be busy. We'll be glad of the rest!"

But the next day, Farmer Brown did come to the farmyard. He passed the big machines and stopped by the little tractor. He used a pail of soapy water to wash her until she shone all over.

"Today I'm going to use YOU, little tractor," he said. "I bought you especially for today's parade. You're going to give rides to all the children in the village!"

All day children queued to get on the little tractor and go for rides. They all agreed that she was the cleanest, prettiest tractor they had ever seen, and she was very careful to drive as smoothly as she could, so her passengers wouldn't feel any lumps or bumps on the road.

"Well done, little tractor," said Farmer Brown. "You are so popular that you can give rides to the children every Saturday. You were a good buy!"

"Hurrah, I've got the best job ever!" thought the little tractor.

That evening, Farmer Brown parked her back alongside the bigger machines in the farmyard. Although she was the smallest tractor, she had by far the biggest smile of them all!

SAM WANTS TO PLAY

One hot summer's day, a little puppy called Sam was born on a farm. He was a very friendly, bouncy puppy who was full of fun.

He liked to play with the little chicks in the henhouse; he let them climb on his back for a ride.

He liked to play with the little lambs in the field; he ran around counting daisies with them.

He liked to play with the little piglets in the farmyard; he rolled about with them in the hay.

But then summer came to an end. Sam didn't really mind; he had fun chasing the autumn leaves But his friends began to stop playing.

The chicks had grown into hens.

"Sorry, we can't play. We're sitting on our eggs," they said. The lambs had grown into sheep.

"Sorry, we can't play. We're busy eating grass," they said. The piglets had grown into pigs.

"Sorry, we can't play. We're just too big!" they said.

Soon snowflakes began to fall, covering the leaves on the ground. Poor Sam had no playmates left, so he played by himself all winter, making pawprints in the snow and counting the snowflakes from the farmhouse window.

Then, bit by bit, the sun began to shine again, and Sam watched his pawprints disappear as the snow melted away and spring arrived.

As soon as the snow had gone, Sam ran to the henhouse to find his old friends.

"Hello, Sam; you've grown," said the hens. "Meet our babies." There, in the henhouse, were lots of new fluffy yellow chicks!

"Do you want to play?" they asked.

"Oh, yes please!" cried Sam.

As soon as he could, Sam ran to the field to find some more of his old friends.

"Hello, Sam; you've grown," said the sheep. "Meet our babies." There, in the field, were lots of new curly white lambs!

"Do you want to play?" they said.

"Oh, yes please!" said Sam.

As soon as he could, Sam ran to the pigpen to find some more of his old friends.

"Hello, Sam; you've grown," said the pigs. "Meet our babies." There, in the pigpen, were lots of new shiny pink piglets!

"Do you want to play?" they asked.

"Oh, yes please!" said Sam. "I may have grown bigger, but I'll ALWAYS want to play. Come on, everyone!" And he danced all around the farmyard, with chicks and lambs and piglets following after him!

THE KING'S NEW FARM

King Michael was very rich. He owned lots of castles, palaces and parks. He even had royal shops, royal playgrounds, royal factories and royal football fields!

One day, he bought a farm to add to his collection. On his orders, the farm was kept spotlessly clean. Every day his servants brushed the animals, polished the floor and swept the farmyard.

The animals were fed from golden buckets and they slept on velvet cushions. The cows had silver collars and the hens had a house in the shape of a castle!

It didn't really look like a proper farm at all, so the animals were very unhappy. They liked lots of mud and straw around them.

The cows did not make much milk, the hens did not lay many eggs and the goose laid no eggs at all!

King Michael was very angry.

"What's wrong with my farm?" he shouted. "I'm going to visit it at once!"

The servants made an extra effort to clean the farm for the visit. They even polished the cows' horns! When King Michael arrived, everything was sparkling.

"I don't think you're milking the cows properly," King Michael said to his servants. "I will show you how to do it."

So King Michael took off his big, round diamond ring and sat down on a milking stool. He handed the ring to a servant, who put it in his pocket.

"I'd like that ring. It looks like a shiny egg," thought the farm goose, and she took it while the servant wasn't looking.

"Where's my ring?" asked King Michael, when he stood up again. He looked round and saw the goose holding it in her beak.

"Get it back!" he shouted.

All the servants chased after the goose – through the fields, through the haybarn and around the milking parlour. They left muddy footprints everywhere!

Then the goose decided to give the ring back, because it was King Michael's, after all. She dropped it in the water trough and the servants had to fish it out with their hats.

"Look at the mess! It will take days to clean up this place," cried King Michael. But the farm animals loved all the mud. They thought it made the farm much cosier!

The very next day, the hens laid extra eggs and the cows made lots of creamy milk.

So the King decided to keep the farm muddy and messy. He was so pleased that he gave the goose a beautiful emerald egg to keep, and from then on the goose gave HIM a big, shiny white egg every morning for his breakfast.

THE LUCKY SHEEP

There was once a market in a big village. All the farmers came to buy and sell their animals. There were cows, pigs, hens, geese – what a noise!

In one corner, sitting in a pen, there were two little sheep. They were feeling very scared.

"Baaa, baaa," they cried, which meant: "What will happen to us?"

Just then a white horse went by.

"Neigh! I'm going to live on a farm by a meadow," he said. "I'm going to pull the plough. Perhaps you will come, too."

"Baaa, baaaa," cried the sheep, which meant: "Oh dear!" They didn't want to pull a plough.

Just then a white goose went by.

"Quack! I'm going to live on a farm by the sea," she said. "I'm going to guard the farmyard. Perhaps you will come, too."

"Baaa, baaaa," cried the sheep, which meant: "Oh dear!" They didn't want to guard a farmyard.

Just then a brown goat went by.

"Bleat! I'm going to live on a farm on a mountain," he said.

"I'm going to wander about in the snow. Perhaps you'll come, too."

"Baaa, baaaa," cried the sheep, which meant: "Oh dear!" They didn't want to wander about in the snow.

The two scared little sheep huddled up in the corner of the pen, so that no-one could see them. But they couldn't keep quiet – "baa, baa!"

Then a kind-looking man peeped over the side of the pen. He wasn't like the other farmers.

"Hello," he said. "I think these sheep are just what I want. I'd like to buy both of them straight away."

"Baaa, baaa, baaa," cried the sheep. They were very frightened! Their new owner led them down the road.

"I haven't got a farm, I'm afraid," he said, and he led them to a house with wide green lawns.

"I'd like you to eat my grass for me. Then I won't have to mow it," he told the little sheep.

"Baaa, baaa," they cried.

"Oh dear, does that mean you don't want to do it?" asked the man.

"Baaa, baaa," they cried, which meant: "Yes, we'd love to. What a perfect home!" They didn't say any more, because they were too busy munching grass!

ALLY AND THE WELL

Not all farms have green fields, tractors and barns full of hay. In very hot countries they are quite different.

Ally was a little boy who lived on a farm in a very hot country. His farm was small; it had two cows and a goat living in the dry and dusty yard outside his house.

Ally helped his parents to milk the animals every day, and he had some of the milk for his breakfast.

In the middle of the yard there was a well. Next to it there was a bucket tied to a long rope, and every day Ally helped his father to drop the bucket down the well and then pull it up full of water.

But one day the bucket came up empty.

"Oh no, the well is dry," cried his father. "We won't have enough water for all the animals! Ally, you will have to take one of the cows over to our neighbour's farm. He has got lots of water there."

Ally felt very sad about taking the cow to the neighbour's farm. The cow was very sad, too. She didn't want to go because she loved Ally very much.

The next day Ally's father dropped the bucket down the well and then pulled it up. Once again, it was empty.

"Ally, you will have to take the other cow to our neighbour's farm," said Father. "We haven't got enough water for her today."

Poor Ally took the other cow to the neighbour, but he didn't really want to.

"Don't worry," he whispered to her softly. "I'll come and fetch you both soon; I know I will!"

Ally missed the cows so much that he couldn't go to sleep that night. He sat outside and watched the beautiful moon, and wished with all his heart that the water would come back into the well.

Then, just as he was about to go indoors, he saw something moving out of the corner of his eye. It was the goat; he was happily chewing the end of the rope that was tied to the bucket!

"Stop it!" cried Ally. He looked at the rope, then he looked at the goat and then he had an idea! He found a pebble and dropped it into the well. It went down a long, long way and then it made a 'splash'.

Ally ran back into his house.

"The well has always been full," he cried. "But the goat has been eating the rope, and he's made it so short that the bucket won't reach the water!"

The next day, Ally's father tied a long new rope to the bucket and pulled it up full to the brim!

Ally ran over to the neighbour's farm to fetch the cows.

"I told you I would come soon," he said. The cows were so pleased to see him that they swished their tails and mooed loudly. They were glad to go home.

After that, the naughty goat got a long new rope of his own. Every evening it was tied from his collar to a tree, so that he couldn't reach the well again, however hungry he felt!